Eating Out: How to Order in Restaurants

Mason Crest
450 Parkway Drive, Suite D
Broomall, PA 19008
www.masoncrest.com

Copyright © 2014 by Mason Crest, an imprint of National Highlights, Inc. All rights reserved. No part of this publication may be reproduced or transmitted in any form or by any means, electronic or mechanical, including photocopying, recording, taping or any information storage and retrieval system, without permission from the publisher.

Printed and bound in the United States of America.

First printing
9 8 7 6 5 4 3 2 1

Series ISBN: 978-1-4222-2874-6
Hardcover ISBN: 978-1-4222-2877-7
ebook ISBN: 978-1-4222-8939-6
Paperback ISBN: 978-1-4222-2987-3

The Library of Congress has cataloged the
    hardcopy format(s) as follows:

Library of Congress Cataloging-in-Publication Data

Etingoff, Kim.
 Eating out : how to order in restaurants / Kim Etingoff.
    pages cm – (Understanding nutrition: a gateway to physical & mental health)
  Audience: Age 10.
  Audience: Grades 4 to 6.
  ISBN 978-1-4222-2877-7 (hardcover) – ISBN 978-1-4222-2874-6 (series) – ISBN 978-1-4222-2987-3 (paperback) – ISBN 978-1-4222-8939-6 (ebook)
 1. Dinners and dining–Juvenile literature. 2. Nutrition–Juvenile literature. 3. Restaurants–Menus–Juvenile literature. I. Title.
 TX355.E85 2014
 642'.5–dc23
                            2013009446

Produced by Vestal Creative Services.
www.vestalcreative.com

UNDERSTANDING NUTRITION:
A GATEWAY TO PHYSICAL AND MENTAL HEALTH

Eating Out:
How to Order in Restaurants

KIM ETINGOFF

Mason Crest

CONTENTS

Introduction	6
1. Healthy Eating in Restaurants	9
2. Choosing Your Restaurant	17
3. Choosing Your Meal	27
4. Eating Out and Staying Healthy	37
Find Out More	46
Index	47
About the Author & Consultant and Picture Credits	48

Introduction
by Dr. Joshua Borus

There are many decisions to make about food. Almost everyone wants to "eat healthy"—but what does that really mean? What is the "right" amount of food and what is a "normal" portion size? Do I need sports drinks if I'm an athlete—or is water okay? Are all "organic" foods healthy? Getting reliable information about nutrition can be confusing. All sorts of restaurants and food makers spend billions of dollars trying to get you to buy their products, often by implying that a food is "good for you" or "healthy." Food packaging has unbiased, standardized nutrition labels, but if you don't know what to look for, they can be hard to understand. Magazine articles and the Internet seem to always have information about the latest fad diets or new "superfoods" but little information you can trust. Finally, everyone's parents, friends, and family have their own views on what is healthy. How are you supposed to make good decisions with all this information when you don't know how to interpret it?

The goal of this series is to arm you with information to help separate what is healthy from not healthy. The books in the series will help you think about things like proper portion size and how eating well can help you stay healthy, improve your mood, and manage your weight. These books will also help you take action. They will let you know some of the changes you can make to keep healthy and how to compare eating options.

Keep in mind a few broad rules:

- First, healthy eating is a lifelong process. Learning to try new foods, preparing foods in healthy ways, and focusing on the big picture are essential parts of that process. Almost no one can keep on a very restrictive diet for a long time or entirely cut out certain groups of foods, so it's best to figure out how to eat healthy in a way that's realistic for you by making a number of small changes.

- Second, a lot of healthy eating hasn't really changed much over the years and isn't that complicated once you know what to look for. The core of a healthy diet is still eating reasonable portions at regular meals. This should be mostly fruits and vegetables, reasonable amounts of proteins, and lots of whole grains, with few fried foods or extra fats. "Junk food" and sweets also have their place—they taste good and have a role in celebrations and other happy events—but they aren't meant to be a cornerstone of your diet!
- Third, avoid drinks with calories in them, beverages like sodas, iced tea, and most juices. Try to make your liquid intake all water and you'll be better off.
- Fourth, eating shouldn't be done mindlessly. Often people will munch while they watch TV or play games because it's something to do or because they're bored rather then because they are hungry. This can lead to lots of extra food intake, which usually isn't healthy. If you are eating, pay attention, so that you are enjoying what you eat and aware of your intake.
- Finally, eating is just one part of the equation. Exercise every day is the other part. Ideally, do an activity that makes you sweat and gets your heart beating fast for an hour a day—but even making small decisions like taking stairs instead of elevators or walking home from school instead of driving make a difference.

After you read this book, don't stop. Find out more about healthy eating. Choosemyplate.gov is a great Internet resource from the U.S. government that can be trusted to give good information; www.hsph.harvard.edu/nutritionsource is a webpage from the Harvard School of Public Health where scientists sort through all the data about food and nutrition and distill it into easy-to-understand messages. Your doctor or nurse can also help you learn more about making good decisions. You might also want to meet with a nutritionist to get more information about healthy living.

Food plays an important role in social events, informs our cultural heritage and traditions, and is an important part of our daily lives. It's not just how we fuel our bodies; it's also but how we nourish our spirit. Learn how to make good eating decisions and build healthy eating habits—and you'll have increased long-term health, both physically and psychologically.

So get started now!

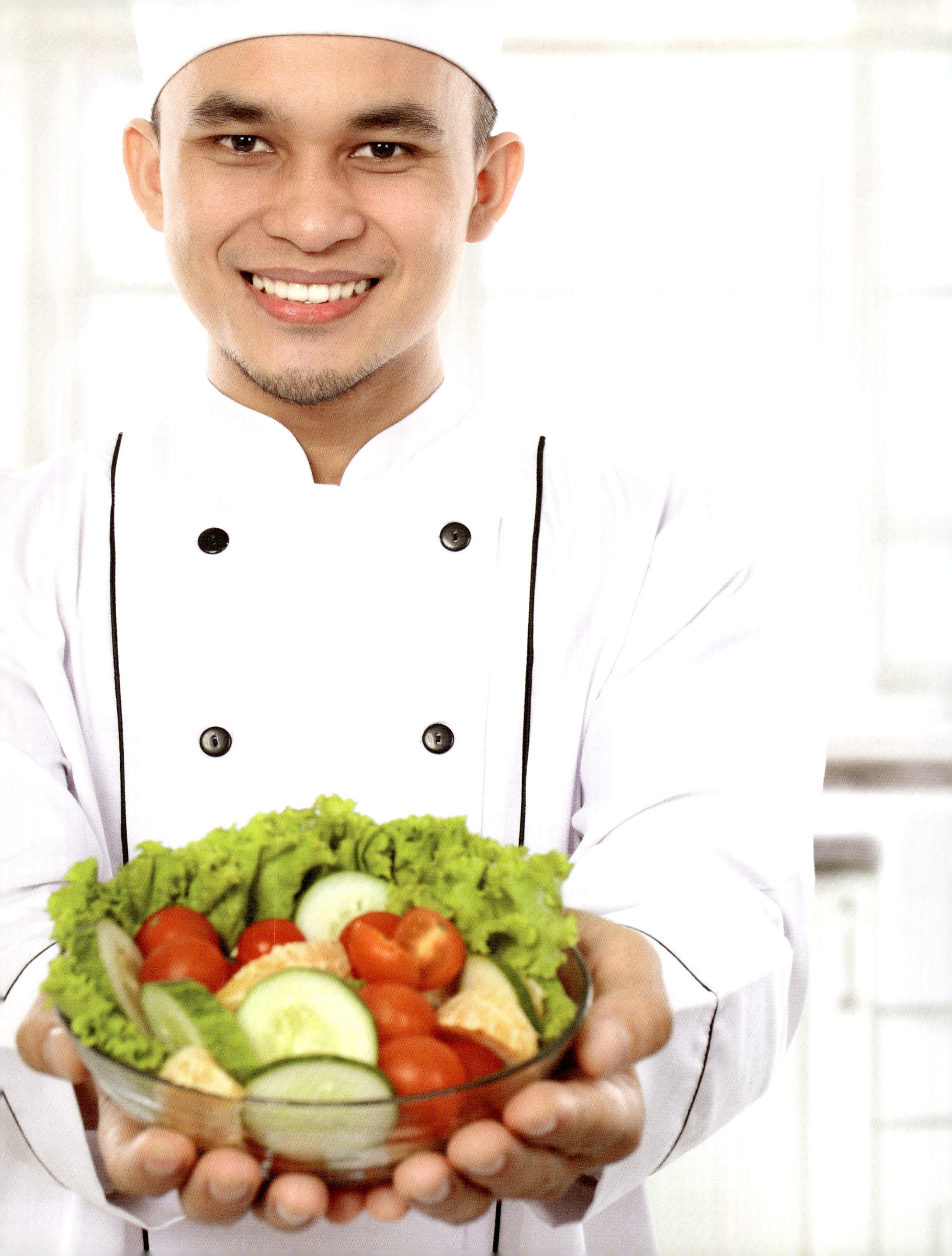

1

Healthy Eating in Restaurants

Think about the last time you went out to eat. Where did you go? What did you eat? How much did you eat? How did you feel afterward?

The answers to these questions have a lot to do with your health. Restaurants are a big part of how we eat, and eating out can be a lot of fun. The danger is when we make unhealthy choices at restaurants. Luckily, there are plenty of ways we can eat out and take care of our health too.

Good Choices

At home, you don't always have much choice about what to eat. Someone else in the family probably does the grocery shopping. You probably don't prepare most of the meals.

At a restaurant, though, you're the one making the choices. You choose what you want to eat and you choose how much you want to eat. You're responsible for making good food choices when you're eating out.

Good food choices mean healthy choices. Food is one of the keys to being healthy. When you eat well, you feel good, you look good, and you don't get sick as often.

If you want to have a healthy **diet**, keep these simple general guidelines in mind. Later on, we'll take a look at what these guidelines mean when you're eating out.

> ### What Does Diet Mean?
>
> When people say they are "going on a **diet**," that means they're going to follow certain rules for how they eat. But when we talk about a healthy diet or an unhealthy diet, we're just referring to the foods you normally eat every day.

- Eat lots of fruits and vegetables.
- Eat whole-grains like brown rice, whole-wheat bread, and oatmeal.
- Eat protein foods without too much fat, like chicken, lean red meat, beans, and tofu.
- Eat small amounts of dairy, like milk, eggs, and cheese.
- Limit how much salt and sugar you eat (and drink).

Dangers

Sometimes eating out gets in the way of eating healthy. We choose the wrong foods or we eat too much food.

Ordering a sandwich with whole-grain bread instead of white can make your lunch a bit healthier. The kind of flour used to make white bread isn't as healthy as whole-wheat flour used to make whole-grain breads.

Healthy Eating in Restaurants 11

Over time, unhealthy food decisions—in restaurants or at home—can have a bad impact on our health. So the sooner you start to eat healthy, the better!

Unhealthy food choices affect a lot of things in our bodies. We have a harder time thinking when we don't have a good diet, and we don't do as well in school or at work. We get tired all the time and don't have the energy to do the things we like to do. We have a harder time moving around as we gain weight. We start to get sick more often. We might even get a serious illness.

What Is Diabetes?

Diabetes is an illness that makes your body unable to use sugar the way it should. Sugar gives us energy to move around. You have something called insulin in your blood, which helps your body use sugar to make that energy. When someone has diabetes, something goes wrong with the insulin.

What Is Cholesterol?

Cholesterol is a waxy substance that's found in certain kinds of fats. Your body needs some cholesterol to build healthy cells, but too much cholesterol can build up in your blood vessels and cause problems with your heart.

Weight gain is often one of the serious consequences of a bad diet. Unhealthy food choices lead to gaining weight. Eating too much over a long time packs on pounds. Weighing too much leads to all sorts of other problems.

Diabetes is one of the big dangers of gaining weight. Today, people are eating more sugar and gaining more weight. As a result, more people are getting diabetes. Even kids are getting diabetes because of the food choices available to them.

People with diabetes have to watch what they eat. Then need to get regular exercise. Diabetes can also lead to serious problems later on, like kidney failure.

Diabetes isn't the only danger from a bad diet. Eating too much salt, **cholesterol**, and fat can lead to heart disease. Too much sugar causes headaches and stomachaches.

By making healthier food choices, you're helping to make sure you avoid a lot of problems later on.

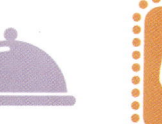

Making unhealthy food choices can lead to weight gain and health problems over time. The food choices you make today can affect you for the rest of your life. Eating right and getting plenty of exercise is the best way to stay healthy as you get older.

Making Eating Out a Healthy Choice

Restaurants aren't bad places. You don't need to give up on eating out because you're afraid of making unhealthy choices. Eating healthy is all about the choices you make when you eat out.

Healthy Eating in Restaurants   13

Description, Analysis is based on one Burger	Calories	Fat (g)
Burger King, Hamburger	333	15
Burger King, Cheeseburger	380	20
Burger King, Cheeseburger, Whopper Jr	460	27
Burger King, Hamburger, Whopper	678	37
Burger King, Cheeseburger, Whopper	790	48
Burger King, Cheeseburger, Double Whopper	1061	68
McDonald's Hamburger	265	10
McDonald's Cheeseburger	313	14
McDonald's Hamburger, Quarter Pounder	417	20
McDonald's Cheeseburger, Big Mac	563	33
McDonald's Cheeseburger, Quarter Pounder, double	734	45
Wendy's, Hamburger, jr	284	10
Wendy's, Hamburger, classic single	464	23
Wendy's, Cheeseburger, classic single	522	27
Wendy's, Hamburger, Big Bacon Classic	570	29
Wendy's, Cheeseburger, classic double	747	44
White Castle, Hamburger, Slyder	140	7
White Castle, Cheeseburger	160	9
White Castle, Cheeseburger, double	290	18
White Castle, Cheeseburger, bacon, double	360	23

Many fast food restaurants serve foods that have a lot of calories in them. One burger can have up to 1,000 calories in it. That's about half of the number of calories a person is meant to eat each day!

EATING OUT: HOW TO ORDER IN RESTAURANTS

Some people go out to eat once in a while. Eating out is a celebration. Restaurants are great places to celebrate. You might go out for a friend's birthday. Or to celebrate the last day of school. Or you and your family might go out for a special meal when you get good grades. If going out to eat at a restaurant is something you only do once in a while, it won't matter so much what you choose to eat when you do eat out.

Other families go out more often, though, like every week or a couple times a week. When you go out so often, you'll need to be a little more careful to make good food choices. Ordering a hamburger and fries every time you go out to eat is not a healthy choice.

You can still eat out every week and order healthy foods. Going out so often can even be a good way to explore different foods. You can find new healthy foods you like by ordering things you've never tried before.

Enjoy the adventure of eating out! You can even go ahead and get that hamburger every once in a while. Just make sure you're trying to eat healthy most of the time, wherever you're eating, whether at home or at a restaurant.

Healthy Eating in Restaurants

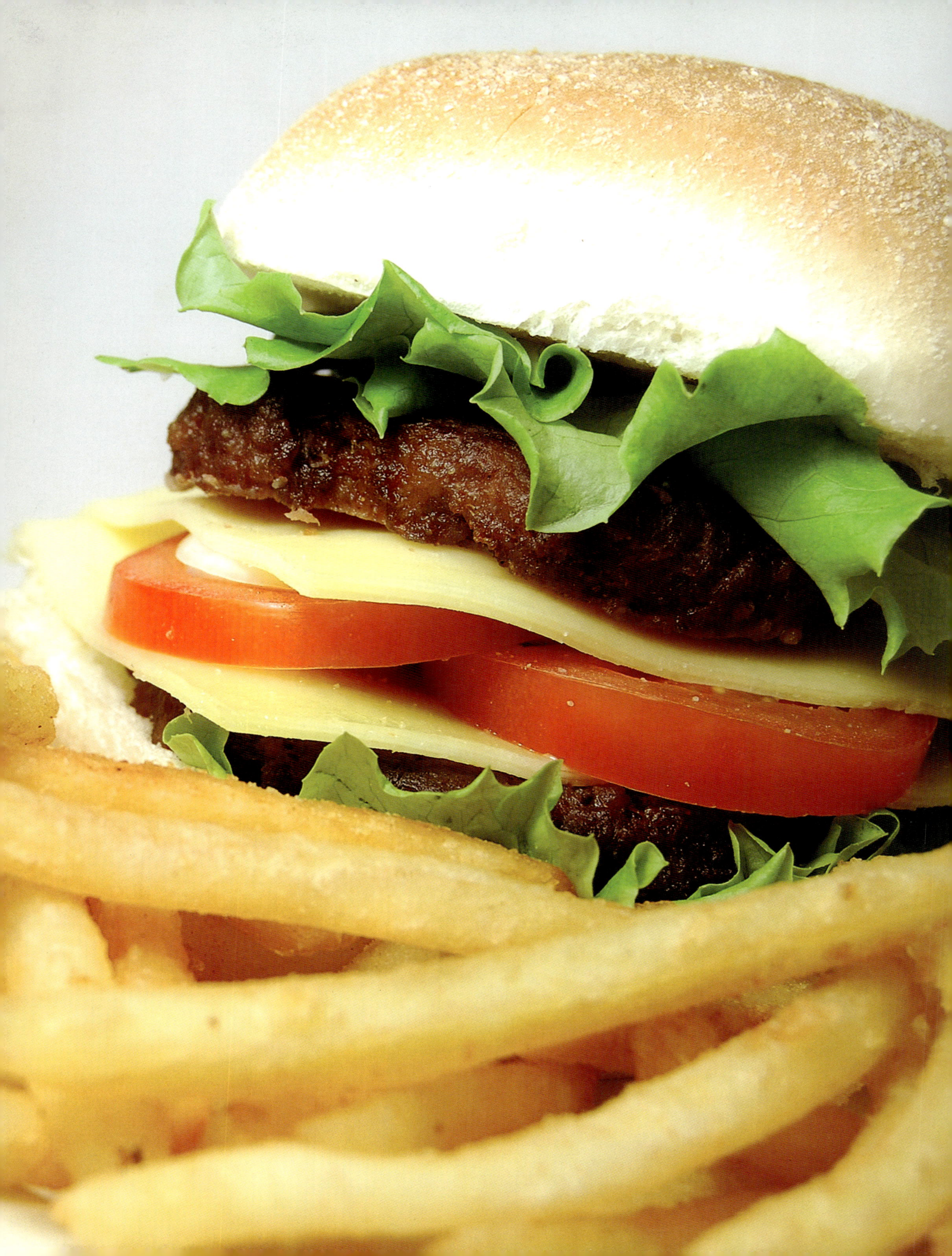

2

Choosing Your Restaurant

Not every restaurant is the same. Some make it a lot easier to make healthy eating choices. Others make it a lot harder. Get smart, and learn which ones are best!

Fast Foods

People eat a lot of fast food. Every day, 50 million people in the United States eat fast food! More than half of everyone in the country eats fast food at least once a week. Some eat it every day. And the numbers are climbing in other parts of the world. McDonald's®

Fast food restaurants like McDonald's make getting food quick and easy, but young people need to be aware of the many unhealthy food choices at these restaurants. Eating burgers, fries, and sodas is all right sometimes, but these foods can be very unhealthy if you eat them too much.

Eating Out: How to Order in Restaurants

and other fast-food restaurants have spread around the world. Fast food is available on every continent of the globe.

Just because so many people eat fast food doesn't mean it's healthy for you. In fact, fast food is some of the unhealthiest food out there.

You can still enjoy your favorite fast-food restaurant sometimes without worrying too much. Try not to go more than once or twice a month if you can help it. Even fewer times is better.

When you do go to fast-food restaurants, you can make better choices. More and more of them are introducing healthier options. In kids' meals, you can get milk and apples. You can order salads with lots of vegetables. You can choose to drink water or 100 percent juice instead of soda.

Whenever you have the choice to order a fruit or vegetables, take it! Keep your meal sizes small or medium. And pass on extra cheese, soda, and mayonnaise.

> **What Does Grilled Mean?**
>
> Something that's been **grilled** is cooked on dry heat with little or no oil added.

Delivery and Takeout

We lead busy lives. Your family probably runs around a lot, working, picking you up from school, taking you to practice. They need some help with meals sometimes when they don't have time to cook. So they order takeout or delivery.

Delivery or takeout means eating restaurant food at home. You have to think about the same health concerns as when you're actually in a restaurant.

A lot of delivery food isn't usually very healthy. Pizzas have a lot of grease (fat) and salt. So do Chinese food and chicken wings.

Talk about some better options with your family. Can someone make food on the weekend and freeze it for dinners during the week? Could you help cook?

When your family does get delivery or takeout, you can make some healthier choices. Choose baked or **grilled** chicken instead of fried. Put extra veggies on your pizza. Anything that adds fruits and vegetables and limits salt, sugar, and fried foods is a good idea!

Choosing Your Restaurant

A grilled chicken breast is a lot healthier than a fried piece of chicken. These kinds of small choices may not seem like a big deal, but all your healthy food choices add up over time.

Eating Out: How to Order in Restaurants

Healthier Delivery and Takeout Food Choices

- Pizza with half cheese and lots of vegetables
- Baked or grilled chicken drumsticks instead of fried
- Steamed Chinese dumplings with brown rice
- Turkey sub with extra vegetables on a whole-wheat roll
- Small hamburger with a side salad

All-You-Can-Eat Buffets

Buffets are a real challenge even for the healthiest eaters! When you're faced with a mountain of food, it's hard to say no.

You can eat as much as you want at buffets. You could eat dessert first. Or only eat fried foods. Or eat five plates full of everything.

Imagine if you ate at buffets every day. You would always be full! You might feel sick. You'd gain weight because you would be eating so much.

Going to buffets is okay once in a while. Save it for a special occasion, though, and don't go more than a few times a year. Eating as much as you possibly can might be fun, but it shouldn't be a habit. You don't want to get used to eating so much.

When you do go to a buffet, make sure you pick some fruits and vegetables. Stay away from too many fried foods and desserts. Drink water instead of soda.

Sit-Down Restaurants

Sit-down restaurants are your best bet for a healthy meal. You usually have a lot of choices at these restaurants. Not every food is filled with lots of salt, sugar, and fat, though some of them definitely are!

Choosing Your Restaurant

Seafood Nutrition Facts

Cooked (by moist or dry heat with no added ingredients), edible weight portion. Percent Daily Values (%DV) are based on a 2,000 calorie diet.

Seafood Serving Size (84 g/3 oz)	Calories	Calories from Fat	Total Fat g / %DV	Saturated Fat g / %DV	Cholesterol mg / %DV	Sodium mg / %DV	Potassium mg / %DV	Total Carbohydrate g / %DV	Protein g	Vitamin A %DV	Vitamin C %DV	Calcium %DV	Iron %DV
Blue Crab	100	10	1 / 2	0 / 0	95 / 32	330 / 14	300 / 9	0 / 0	20g	0%	4%	10%	4%
Catfish	130	60	6 / 9	2 / 10	50 / 17	40 / 2	230 / 7	0 / 0	17g	0%	0%	0%	0%
Clams, about 12 small	110	15	1.5 / 2	0 / 0	80 / 27	95 / 4	470 / 13	6 / 2	17g	10%	0%	8%	30%
Cod	90	5	1 / 2	0 / 0	50 / 17	65 / 3	460 / 13	0 / 0	20g	0%	2%	2%	2%
Flounder/Sole	100	15	1.5 / 2	0 / 0	55 / 18	100 / 4	390 / 11	0 / 0	19g	0%	0%	2%	0%
Haddock	100	10	1 / 2	0 / 0	70 / 23	85 / 4	340 / 10	0 / 0	21g	2%	0%	2%	6%
Halibut	120	15	2 / 3	0 / 0	40 / 13	60 / 3	500 / 14	0 / 0	23g	4%	0%	2%	6%
Lobster	80	0	0.5 / 1	0 / 0	60 / 20	320 / 13	300 / 9	1 / 0	17g	2%	0%	6%	2%
Ocean Perch	110	20	2 / 3	0.5 / 3	45 / 15	95 / 4	290 / 8	0 / 0	21g	0%	2%	10%	4%
Orange Roughy	80	5	1 / 2	0 / 0	20 / 7	70 / 3	340 / 10	0 / 0	16g	2%	0%	4%	2%
Oysters, about 12 medium	100	35	4 / 6	1 / 5	80 / 27	300 / 13	220 / 6	6 / 2	10g	0%	6%	6%	45%
Pollock	90	10	1 / 2	0 / 0	80 / 27	110 / 5	370 / 11	0 / 0	20g	2%	0%	0%	2%
Rainbow Trout	140	50	6 / 9	2 / 10	55 / 18	35 / 1	370 / 11	0 / 0	20g	4%	4%	8%	2%
Rockfish	110	15	2 / 3	0 / 0	40 / 13	70 / 3	440 / 13	0 / 0	21g	4%	0%	2%	2%
Salmon, Atlantic/Coho/Sockeye/Chinook	200	90	10 / 15	2 / 10	70 / 23	55 / 2	430 / 12	0 / 0	24g	4%	4%	2%	2%
Salmon, Chum/Pink	130	40	4 / 6	1 / 5	70 / 23	65 / 3	420 / 12	0 / 0	22g	2%	0%	2%	4%
Scallops, about 6 large or 14 small	140	10	1 / 2	0 / 0	65 / 22	310 / 13	430 / 12	5 / 2	27g	2%	0%	4%	14%
Shrimp	100	10	1.5 / 2	0 / 0	170 / 57	240 / 10	220 / 6	0 / 0	21g	4%	4%	6%	10%
Swordfish	120	50	6 / 9	1.5 / 8	40 / 13	100 / 4	310 / 9	0 / 0	16g	2%	2%	0%	6%
Tilapia	110	20	2.5 / 4	1 / 5	75 / 25	30 / 1	360 / 10	0 / 0	22g	0%	2%	0%	4%
Tuna	130	15	1.5 / 2	0 / 0	50 / 17	40 / 2	480 / 14	0 / 0	26g	2%	2%	2%	4%

Seafood is often a very healthy choice when eating out. Fish is a good source of protein and doesn't have much bad fat in it either.

Eating Out: How to Order in Restaurants

Sit-down restaurants will usually have many healthy choices on the menu. You'll still have to think about the foods you're ordering, but many restaurants make picking healthy food easy. Some even have different menus for people who want to order healthier foods.

You can choose from all kinds of sit-down restaurants. Which ones are best? Try to visit ones that serve lots of vegetables. Steakhouses aren't the best choice to go to regularly. Restaurants that only serve fried chicken aren't either.

Eat at restaurants that have a lot of variety on their menus. You'll be able to pick and choose exactly what you want to eat. Chances are, you can find a couple of healthy items on the menu.

A big problem in restaurants is that people eat too much. Serving sizes are often much bigger than what you would normally have at home. But you can always take home with you whatever food you don't eat. Only eat until you are full.

Choosing Your Restaurant

By ordering whole-wheat pasta, you can make many Italian dishes a bit healthier when you go out. Many people won't even be able to tell the difference, making whole-wheat pasta an easy, healthy choice.

Ethnic Foods

Depending on where you live, you can find restaurants that serve all kinds of food! Ethnic food restaurants offer some healthy choices, if you know how to order well.

Ethnic restaurants serve food that is based on traditions from other countries. People around the world today enjoy Italian food, Chinese food, and Mexican food. Thai food and Indian food are becoming more popular too. More new restaurants are opening up, like Afghani and Ethiopian restaurants.

Many ethnic restaurants serve up choices with a lot of veggies. Thai dishes, for example, often have carrots, peppers, broccoli, corn, bamboo shoots, and more.

However, you can't order just anything from a menu and assume it's healthy. Ethnic restaurants serve plenty of less healthy foods. Italian restaurants have pastas covered in cream sauce. Chinese food generally has a lot of salt in it. Indian restaurants serve fried foods and food with lots of butter. But choose wisely, and you can have a healthy meal!

More Healthy Food By Restaurant

Try these options:

- Italian: whole-wheat pasta, tomato sauces, salad with Italian dressing, minestrone soup
- Mexican: salsa, soft tacos rather than fried taco shells, fajitas, rice, one serving of guacamole
- Steakhouses: sirloin, tenderloin, green salad with vinaigrette; eat only 3 to 6 ounces of meat (about the size of two decks of cards)

Choosing Your Restaurant

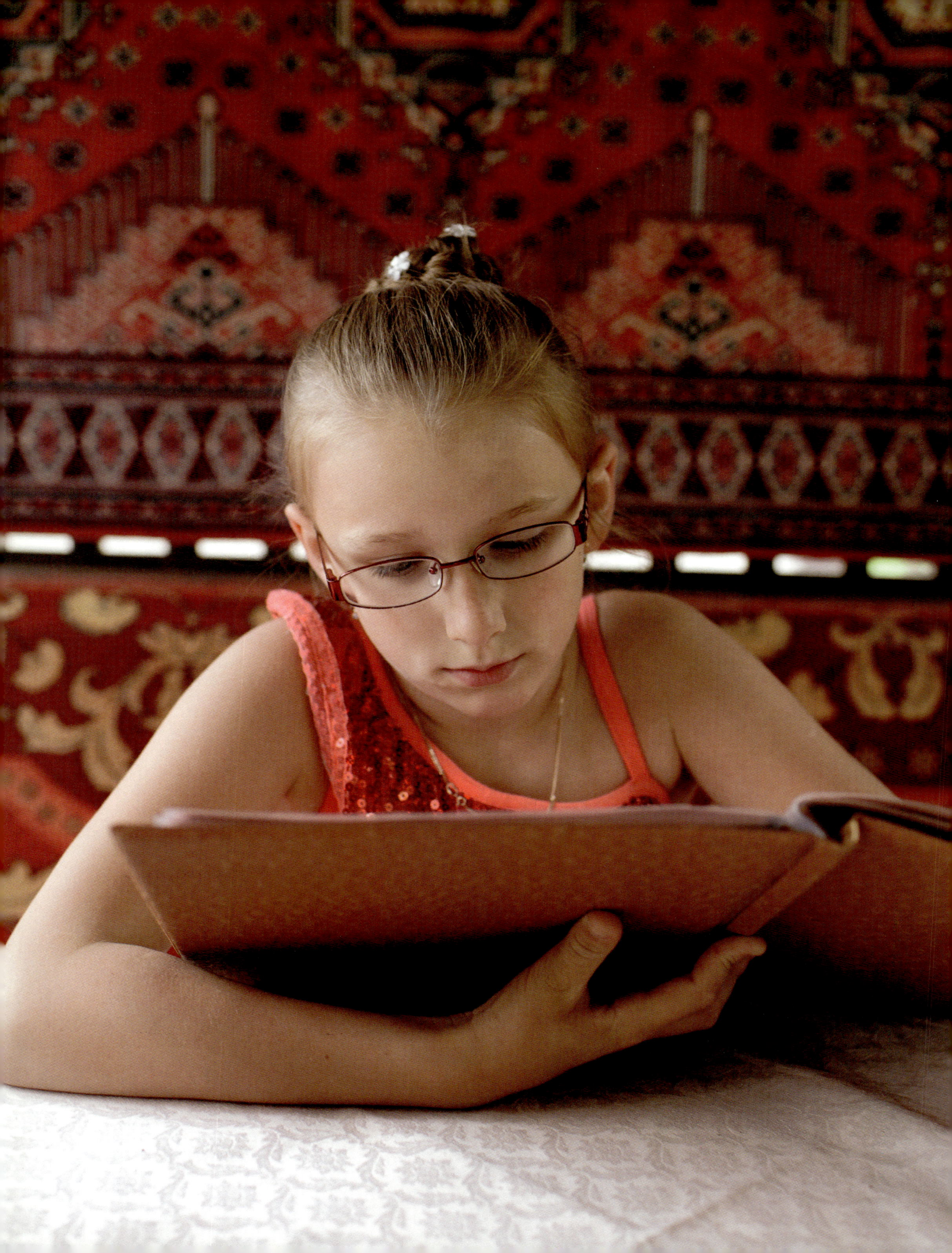

3

Choosing Your Meal

Eating healthy in any restaurant is possible. You just have to know a few tricks.

Choosing Healthy Foods

Guidelines for healthy eating are exactly the same at home and at a restaurant. First, you want to eat as many fruits and vegetables as possible. Restaurants usually offer at least some kind of fruit or veggie. It's up to you to order it!

GOOD	BAD
BROILED	FRIED
STEAMED	BATTERED
BLACKENED	BUTTERY
BAKED	CREAMY
ROASTED	CRISPY
LIGHT	CHEESY
FRESH	THICK
GRILLED	BREADED
SAUTEED	SMOTHERED

Sometimes the words on the menu can tell you whether a food is healthy or not. Watch for words that might mean extra salt, sugar, or fat.

Many dishes come with a choice of French fries or something else. Check out that something else—it might be a vegetable side like a salad or soup with veggies. Some kids' menus might have apple slices or carrot sticks. When you're craving fries, see if you can order half fries and half of the vegetable side.

EATING OUT: HOW TO ORDER IN RESTAURANTS

Pick main dishes that have lots of fruit and veggies in them. What's better: pancakes with syrup and whipped cream or waffles with fresh strawberries? A cheeseburger or a stir-fry with carrots and broccoli? The answer is also the food that contains fresh fruits or vegetables. Strawberries, carrots, and broccoli are great things to eat.

Do you see any whole grains on the menu? Some places might let you choose brown rice instead of white rice. Or whole-wheat toast instead of white toast. When you have those options, take them.

> ## What Do Broiled and Steamed Mean?
>
> Food that has been **broiled** has been cooked with very high heat, usually with little or no added oil. Food that has been **steamed** has been cooked using steam (very hot moisture), which adds no extra calories to the food.

Restaurants have a lot of fried things, like french fries, chicken nuggets, fried fish, and onion rings. Fried foods are something you probably don't eat very often at home, but they're common in restaurants. They taste good, but fried foods have a lot of fat in them. They also have a ton of calories. You can eat fried foods once in a while as a treat, but as often as you can, try to make other menu choices.

Choose alternatives to fried foods. Lots of restaurants have other options. Look for the words "baked," "**broiled**," "**steamed**," or "grilled." All those choices are tasty. Baked foods even give you the same crunch as fried. Instead of fried chicken, get baked chicken. Instead of fried dumplings, get steamed dumplings.

One of the simplest choices you can make when you're eating out is to not drink soda. Soda has a lot of sugar in it and not much else. Replace soda with water or juice when you're out to eat. Restaurants usually have some good choices. Try bubbly water if you want something fizzy!

What about dessert? Sometimes you just have to have something sweet at the end of a meal. See if the restaurant has fresh fruit. Yogurt and fruit is a good option. When you do order a special dessert, try to pick one with fruit in it. Cake and pie aren't the healthiest options, but if you choose banana cake or apple pie, you're at least getting a little fruit!

Choosing Your Meal

1 Serving Looks Like . . .

GRAIN PRODUCTS

1 cup of cereal flakes = fist

1 pancake = compact disc

½ cup of cooked rice, pasta, or potato = ½ baseball

1 slice of bread = cassette tape

1 piece of cornbread = bar of soap

1 Serving Looks Like . . .

VEGETABLES AND FRUIT

1 cup of salad greens = baseball

1 baked potato = fist

1 med. fruit = baseball

½ cup of fresh fruit = ½ baseball

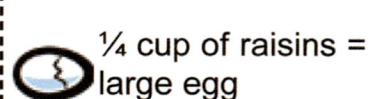

¼ cup of raisins = large egg

1 Serving Looks Like . . .

DAIRY AND CHEESE

1½ oz. cheese = 4 stacked dice or 2 cheese slices

½ cup of ice cream = ½ baseball

FATS

1 tsp. margarine or spreads = 1 dice

1 Serving Looks Like . . .

MEAT AND ALTERNATIVES

3 oz. meat, fish, and poultry = deck of cards

3 oz. grilled/baked fish = checkbook

2 Tbsp. peanut butter = ping pong ball

Knowing serving sizes is a good way to make sure you don't eat too much. This chart can help you remember some serving sizes and keep your portions under control.

30 EATING OUT: HOW TO ORDER IN RESTAURANTS

More Tips

- Ask for salad dressing on the side, so that you can control how much you put on your salad. Get vinaigrette or Italian (which have less fat) instead of ranch or blue cheese (which have a lot of fat).
- Order low-fat milk instead of whole milk.
- Pick broth-based soups (like chicken noodle) instead of creamy soups (like clam chowder).
- When you get pizza, add some vegetables on top.
- When you get free bread or tortilla chips before a meal, only eat a little.
- Choose tomato sauces on your pasta instead of creamy alfredo.

Portion Control

Just about everyone has eaten way too much at a restaurant. You see that mound of food, and you can't help but eat it all! Eating all that food doesn't feel that great afterward, though. Remember that sick feeling the next time you go out to eat and want to eat too much. You don't have to eat until you feel sick.

When you have a choice of meal size, choose small or medium. Stay away from menu choices that use the words jumbo, deluxe, super, giant, or extra-large. You won't be tempted to overeat when you only have a smaller amount of food on your plate.

You could also decide to order a salad first every time you go out to eat. The very first thing you'll eat is filled with lots of veggies. Then, move on to your main meal. You'll get full before you can eat the whole thing.

Choosing Your Meal